MY BOOK!

THIS BOOK BELONGS TO

Bowling

IF YOU SHOULD FIND MY BOOK,

PLEASE RETURN IT TO ME.

THANK YOU!

NAME _____

STREET _____

CITY _____

STATE _____ **ZIP** _____

DEAR PARENTS,

Welcome to *Travels With MAX to Washington, D.C.*! Endorsed by teachers and parents, this book reinforces the philosophy that "fun is learning and learning is fun." With the assistance of their guide, MAX, children solve puzzles, laugh at silly riddles, and color pictures as they tour the capital of the United States.

When the capital tour ends, the fun continues for kids. They are now eligible to join MAX's **VIK (Very Important Kid) Club**. As soon as children send MAX their Frequent Reader Coupon, he will mail them their **VIK** card. This card makes children official members of his club, and enables them to receive lots of MAX surprises. The Coupon and MAX's address can be found on page 47.

Giving *Travels With MAX* to children prior to visiting Washington, D.C., is the perfect gift to prepare them for this exciting and educational trip. For children who are unable to visit the nation's capital, receiving this book is the next best thing! Written for parents too, this book includes a **Parent Guide** which lists pertinent information for many attractions that families will want to visit.

Travels With MAX to Washington, D.C., is part of a four-book series written on the nation's capital. To receive more information about this series and the other cities that MAX has traveled to, please call MAX's toll free number at **1-800-4-MAX-008**. Now, on with the tour!

Thank you for traveling with us,

Nancy Ann VanWie

Nancy Ann Van Wie, M.Ed., and MAX!
Authors

No portion of this book may be reproduced without written permission from the publisher. Printed in the U.S.A.

ISBN 0-9626206-1-0
ALL RIGHTS RESERVED

ILLUSTRATOR: KARI MOE
PUBLISHER: MAX'S PUBLICATIONS

COPYRIGHT © 1993
1-800-4-MAX-008

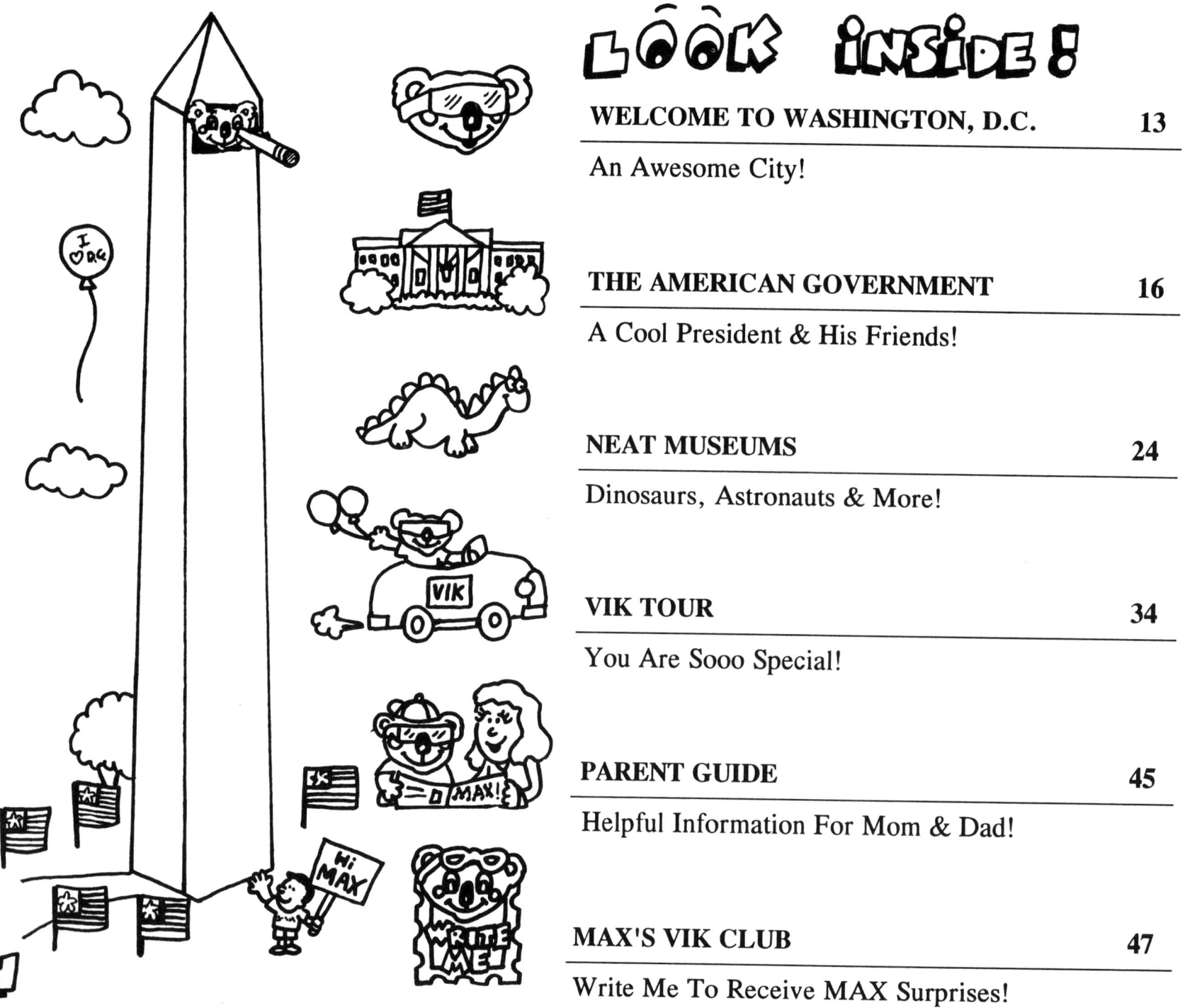

LOOK INSIDE!

WELCOME TO WASHINGTON, D.C.	**13**
An Awesome City!	
THE AMERICAN GOVERNMENT	**16**
A Cool President & His Friends!	
NEAT MUSEUMS	**24**
Dinosaurs, Astronauts & More!	
VIK TOUR	**34**
You Are Sooo Special!	
PARENT GUIDE	**45**
Helpful Information For Mom & Dad!	
MAX'S VIK CLUB	**47**
Write Me To Receive MAX Surprises!	

MAX'S TRAVEL TIPS!

 **Always wear your seat belt** and make sure that your brothers and sisters, parents, and everyone else is **buckled-up for safety!**

 **Do not talk to strangers.** Stay close to your brothers and sisters, parents, and friends at all times.

 **Always be polite** and obey all rules. Cross the street only when the stop light says "walk." Throw your litter only in a litter basket.

 **Memorize your name**, telephone number and address. Before your trip, discuss with your parents what you would do if you got lost. **Remember Mate:**

It's Cool To Follow The Rules!

TRAVELS WITH MAX!

Good Day, Mate. My name is MAX!

I am a **VIK** (Very Important Koala)! I travel all over the world visiting fun places and interviewing famous people.

Because I am a **VIK**, the President of the United States called to say that he wants to meet me. Awesome!

So here I am traveling to Washington, D.C., with my assistant, Birdie. Soon we will meet the President and tour the capital of the United States. Are you ready to have fun?

Then follow me, Mate!

FUN THINGS 2 DO!

As we travel from page to page, there are pictures to color, puzzles to solve, riddles to laugh at, and brain teasers to prove how smart you are! Plus, there is your very own travel diary, so you will always remember the fun things we did in Washington, D.C.!

After our travels, you can join my **VIK** (Very Important Kid) Club. To receive your **VIK card**, return the Frequent Reader Coupon. It's on page 47. Now Mate, on with the tour!

HERE IS WASHINGTON, D.C.!

Washington, D.C. is located on the East Coast, between the states of Maryland and Virginia. Today, Washington, D.C. is one of the most beautiful and important cities in the world!

In 1791, over 200 years ago, George Washington, first President of the United States, hired a French architect named Pierre L'Enfant to design a city where the federal government would be located. In 1800, Washington, D.C. was named the **capital of the United States!**

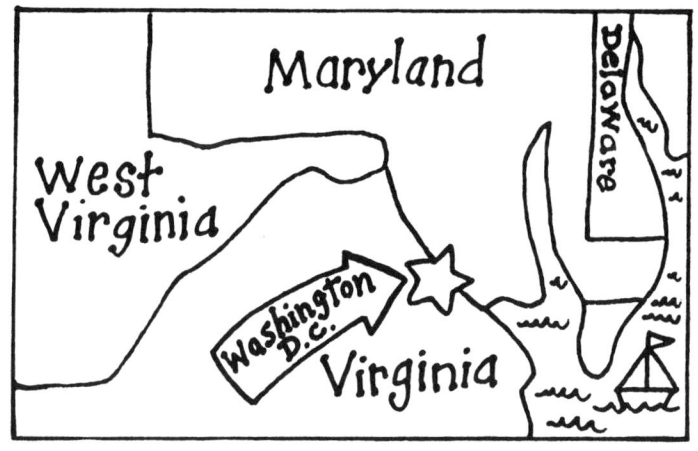

Oui (wē), Oui (wē), Monsieur (mē syû) Washington. For you, I will design a totally awesome city!

Follow the picture clues to see where Pierre L'Enfant was born!

WHERE DO YOU LIVE?

Find the star on the map. This is where Washington, D.C. is located. Where do you live? _____

If you live in the United States, can you find your state? Color your state red. If you have friends or relatives that live in other states, try to find those states on the map and color those states yellow.

MAX'S FACTS!
Did you know that Washington, D.C. (D.C. stands for District of Columbia) is the only city or town in America that is not part of a state?!

I LIVE HERE!

I live in Australia which is halfway around the world from Washington, D.C.

My country is often called "down under" because Australia lies south of the equator. The United States lies north of the equator.

Do you live north or south of the equator? On a map or globe, ask your parents to show you where Australia is and where you live.

O.K. Mate, get your suitcase out, it is time to pack for Washington, D.C.!

What's green, has two legs and a trunk?

A seasick tourist!

MAX'S FACTS!
Seasons in Australia are opposite those in the United States. When it is winter in the United States, it is summer in Australia.

PACKED 2 THE MAX!

Here I am Mate, all packed for our trip. Depending on the time of year you visit D.C., you will need to pack different kinds of clothes. Two things you also need to pack: your MAX book and your toothbrush!

My mom's on my case. She said I packed too much. In the picture below, can you find the 12 things she made me put back in my bedroom? Good luck!!

| hammer | flower | light bulb | pencil | heart | phone | hanger |
| safety pin | comb | milk carton | band aid | paint brush |

D.C., HERE WE COME!!!

Thanks for your help, Mate. Now that we are all packed, we are ready to travel to Washington, D.C. If I could take a pretend trip, I would travel by dinosaur. How would you travel? _____

HERE ARE MORE FUN WAYS TO TRAVEL!

Below are 10 hidden words. Can you find them? Look up, down and across. Good luck, Mate!

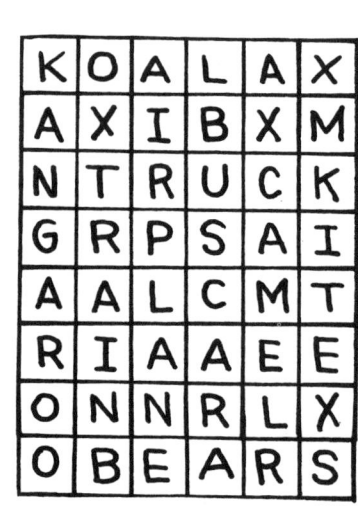

K	O	A	L	A	X
A	X	I	B	X	M
N	T	R	U	C	K
G	R	P	S	A	I
A	A	L	C	M	T
R	I	A	A	E	E
O	N	N	R	L	X
O	B	E	A	R	S

Hurrah! We are here. I am so excited. This is such an awesome city!

There's the President's helicopter. He flew back to D.C. just for our meeting. I don't want to be late, so I better look at my map to find out how to get to the White House. For the coolest map you will ever see, turn the page, Mate!

MAX'S FACTS!
Washington, D.C. was named after the first President of the U.S., George Washington!

First Stop, White House!

On my map, you saw a few of the awesome places we will visit. **First stop is the White House!** Did you find it? That's right Mate, it's on Pennsylvania Avenue!

Now, how do we get there? We could travel by car, taxi, bus, bicycle or skateboard, but I think we should take the Metrorail, or the "Metro" as the "in" crowd calls it.

The Metro is a fast, clean and fun subway system. Riding the Metro is also easy! First, read the map to see where you will go, what color subway to take and how much it will cost. Then, put your money in the machine and your ticket will pop out! Remember: Metro lines have 4 colors: red, blue, yellow and orange. If you have questions, ask the nice people in the information booth.

O.K. Mate, it's time to take the Metro to the White House!

AN AWESOME HOUSE!

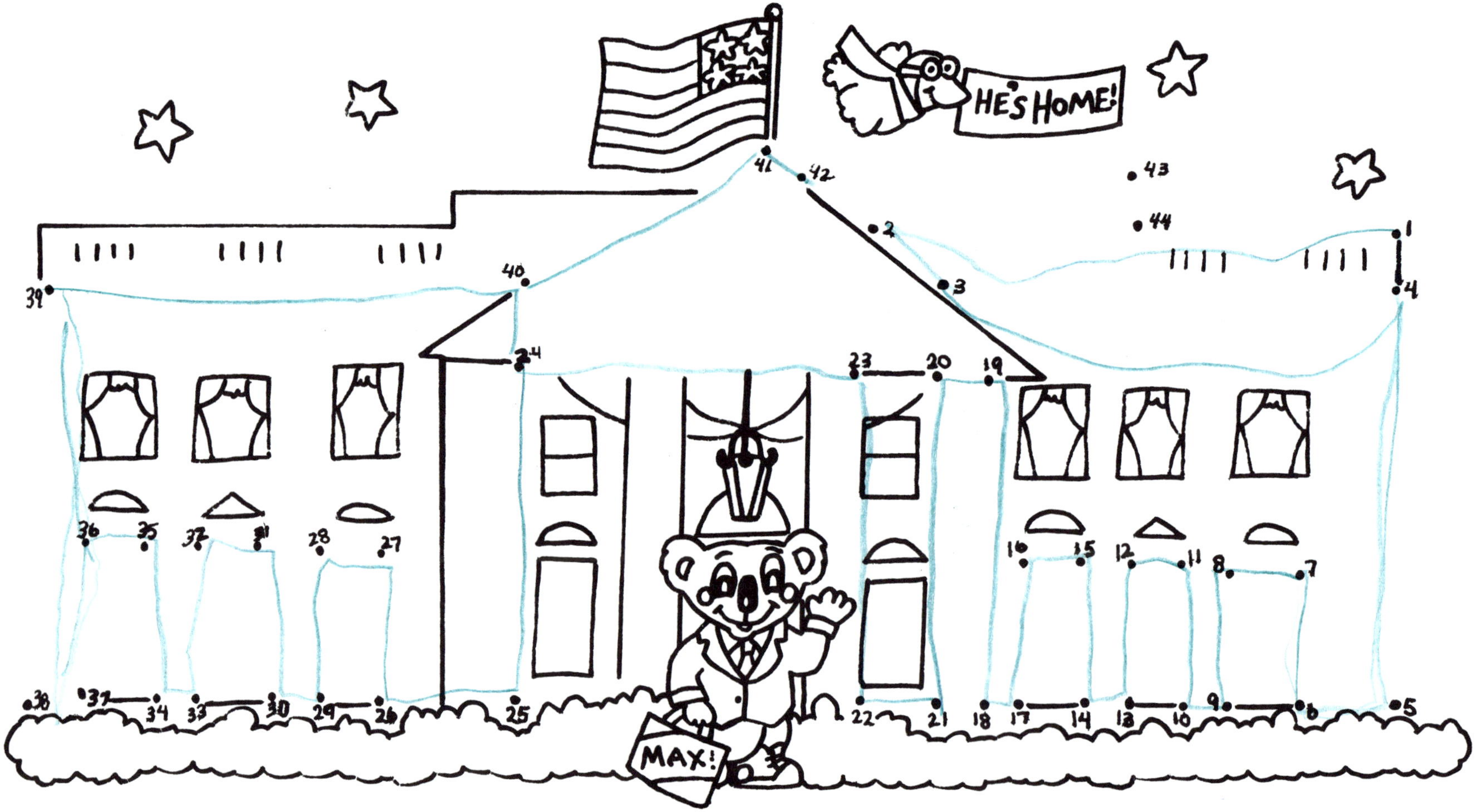

This is it: **1600 Pennsylvania Avenue, Washington, D.C. 20500**, the most famous address in the U.S. I see the flag is flying from the rooftop of the White House. That means the President is home.

And, I am ready to meet the President! In my briefcase, I have an autographed MAX book for him, paper and pencil, and my calculator. I don't understand all this talk about the budget deficit. How BIG is it? I hope he can show me on my calculator. O.K., here I go. I am so nervous. I know I am famous, but so is he. Do you think the President is nervous to meet me? **Wish me luck, Mate!**

A COOL PRESIDENT!

Wow, meeting the President was awesome! He is sooo cool! He gave me a tour, answered my questions and told me lots of interesting facts.

Did you know that George Washington is the only President who has not lived in the White House? He died one year before it was finished.

I also learned that **the White House was first called the President's House**. Built out of sandstone, white paint was added to waterproof the stone. Because of its color, people started calling it the White House.

While lounging at the pool, he told me that **the White House has 132 rooms!** There's a bowling alley, 34 bathrooms, an outdoor and indoor swimming pool, a small movie theatre, and lots more! Sorry Mate, you won't see these on your White House tour, but 6 rooms you will visit are listed below.

Before we said good-bye, we also talked about how we love children and think it is so important they have books to read. Then, the President thanked me for his MAX book and said he hopes lots of kids come to D.C. So Mate, when you visit the White House, tell the President, MAX says hi!!!

CAN YOU PUT THESE 6 WHITE HOUSE ROOMS IN ALPHABETICAL ORDER? GOOD LUCK!

Green Room   **Blue Room**   **Red Room**   **East Room**   **State Dining Room**   **China Room**

1._____   4._____

2._____   5._____

3._____   6._____

THE CAPITOL!

It's off to the Capitol! From the White House, we travel southeast down Pennsylvania Avenue. On page 14, can you trace our route to the Capitol?

Here it is! This huge building with a statue of a woman on top of it (called the Statue of Freedom) is where Congress meets to make laws. Congress is made up of Senators and Representatives. From each state, there are 2 Senators. Name your state's Senators:

1._____ 2._____

The House of Representatives has 435 members. The number of Representatives each state has depends on that state's population. Do you know how many Representatives your state has? _____

MAX'S FACTS!
Taking a tour of the Capitol is awesome! You will visit famous rooms including Statuary Hall! This is the room with the "echo." Ask your guide to show you where it is and then play a trick on your parents Tell them to whisper something. When you know the answer, they will be so surprised!

JUDGES 'N BOOKS!

Across the street from the Capitol is the highest court in the land, the **Supreme Court**! There are 9 judges, called justices. They are appointed by the President. Unlike the President who runs for office every four years, a Supreme Court justice is appointed for life. In 1790 the first Court met and for the next 191 years, all of the justices were men. But in 1981 Sandra Day O'Connor was appointed the first female Supreme Court justice! If you want to see the Supreme Court "in action," call ahead to find out what days it is in session.

Next door to the Supreme Court is the **Library of Congress**. This is the nation's largest library! Sorry Mate, this is not a library where you and I can check out books, but instead, it is a research library for Congress. This Library of Congress has other duties. It also serves as the nation's "copyright headquarters." To protect a book from being copied, the Library of Congress registers the copyright. If you look on page 3, the lower right side, you will see proof of my copyright. It's very cool!

Let's go visit my friends in the Copyright Office at the Library of Congress. Can you help me find it?

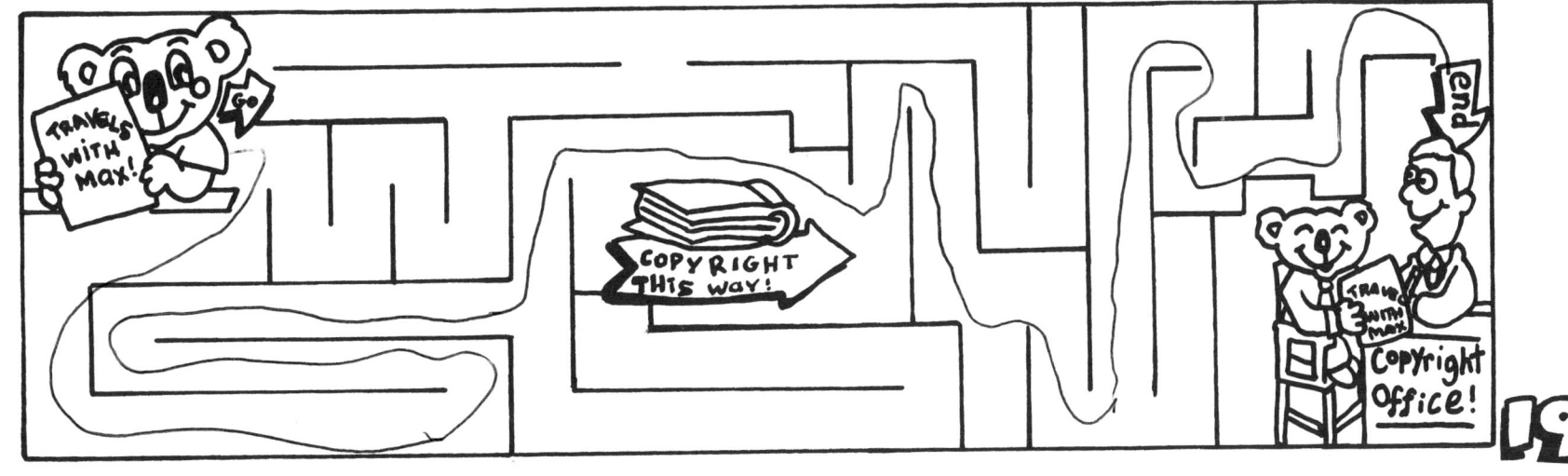

POLITICAL PARTIES

Here are a few more things I learned about the the American government. To become a Senator, a Representative or the President, Americans vote for the candidate of their choice.

Every man and woman who is an American citizen and at least 18 years old, has the right to vote. When will you be able to vote?

```
  18    (voting age)
-  ___   (your age)
        (more years)
```

Voting is very special. There are people in other parts of the world who do not have the freedom to vote like Americans do. Voting is also fun! You get to go behind a curtain and vote secretly!

When you vote for candidates, you are voting for their political party. The 2 main political parties are Democrats and Republicans. The donkey is the symbol of the Democratic Party and the elephant is the symbol of the Republican Party. Today, the President of the United States is President _____ _____. The President is a Democrat or Republican. (Circle the answer).

 Now, ask your parents what political party they belong to and circle their answer!

MY MOM IS A   _DEMOCRAT_   OR   _REPUBLICAN_

MY DAD IS A   _REPUBLICAN_   OR   _DEMOCRAT_

PRESIDENT'S PLEDGES!

Meeting the President and learning about the American government was awesome! If I were President of the United States, here are **3 things I would do**!

1. I would make sure that all children went to bed with hugs and kisses, a full tummy and lots of books to read!

2. Everyone would work with the elderly and help save our Planet Earth by recycling and being kind to animals!

3. And, I would pledge that 1 day a week, kids (and koalas) could eat all the pizza and ice cream they wanted to. Yesss!

Spell what the President sees every day!

H _ T _ H U _ E

As President, what 3 things would you do?

1. _____
   _____

2. _____
   _____

3. _____
   _____

Without peeking, here are a few questions to test your brain power. **Circle your answer**. When you finish, turn to the page listed at the end of each question to see how you did. **Have fun Mate, and good luck!**

1. When the President is home the:
   Curtains are closed   OR   The flag flies from the White House rooftop   (Page 16)

2. The symbol for the Democratic Party is the:
   Whale   OR   Elephant   OR   Donkey   OR   Dinosaur   (Page 20)

3. The statue on top of the Capitol is the Statue of Freedom and it is a:
   Flower   OR   Woman   OR   Horse   OR   Koala   (Page 18)

4. To vote you must be an American citizen and at least:
   10 years old   OR   21 years old   OR   18 years old   (Page 20)

5. The architect from France who designed Washington D.C. is:
   Monsieur Ronald McDonald   OR   Pierre L'Enfant   (Page 8)

6. The symbol for the Republican Party is the:
   Donkey   OR   Kangaroo   OR   Elephant   OR   Shark   (Page 20)

7. The White House was first named the:
   House of Presidents   OR   House of Pancakes   OR   President's House   (Page 17)

 **Yesss! You are sooo smart! Now, it's off to see more money than you have ever seen!**

$ MONEY $ MONEY $

Here we are! **The Bureau of Engraving and Printing** is so cool! You will see money being printed right in front of your eyes. Sorry Mate, no free samples!

Shall we design our own money? Here is mine!

Now, design what your money would look like!

MAX'S FACTS!
Money is not made from paper, but from a special cloth that is 75% cotton and 25% linen.

Martha Washington is the only woman who ever appeared on United States paper money.

On the $1 bill, there used to be a picture of the U.S. national bird - the bald eagle. Now, George Washington's picture is on it.

NEAT MUSEUMS!

Now, it's off to the museums. They are so neat. You get to see fun things and learn interesting facts. Today, we are going to visit the largest museum complex in the world - the **Smithsonian Institution**!

More than just 1 museum, it is 14 museums and the National Zoo! There is so much to see and do, so your first stop should be the Smithsonian Institution Building or the "Castle" as the "in" people call it. Here you will find out what's happening at the museums.

On our museum tour, you will learn about animals and insects from all over the world, airplanes, astronauts and rockets, the American flag, and more! Remember Mate: Do NOT leave the museums until you check out their awesome bookstores. **Now, it's off to the first museum. Can you find it?**

☆ STARS 'N STRIPES

Wow, at the National Museum of American History, you can see the **Star-Spangled Banner!** In 1814, this is the flag that Francis Scott Key wrote a poem about. Those words were put to music and today, that song is the U.S. national anthem.

Now, you must visit the **Hands On History Room!** There are over 40 activities you can do. Send a telegram, harness a mule, make a rope and more!

At this neat museum you will also see the "swinging pendulum," covered wagons, gowns worn by First Ladies, and lots more! Have fun, Mate!

MAX'S FACTS!
Who made the 1st American flag? No one knows for sure, but many people think Betsy Ross did.

What did Betsy Ross say when her cat scared her?

Oh, my stars!

25

A B-I-G MUSEUM!

The National Museum of Natural History is so big! There are over 120 million (yes, 120 million) objects here! First, you will see an African Bush Elephant. Did you know that the African Bush Elephant is the largest land animal in the world today? They are vegetarians (no meat in their diet, Mate)! They eat 18 hours a day (wow, no wonder they are so big) and they have huge brains! Just pick up the phone to learn more interesting facts. **Now, let's visit more of this b-i-g museum!**

FUN THiNGS 2 DO!

Like dinosaurs? Then it's off to the **Dinosaur Gallery** where you will see dinosaurs, dinosaur eggs, prehistoric bones and more. It's awesome!

And, if you visit the **Gem Hall** you will see the Hope Diamond. This diamond is 45.5 carats which makes it the world's largest blue diamond. Wow, that's big!

Then, at the **Insect Zoo**, you can watch ants, beetles, tarantulas and other insects as they eat, crawl and sleep!

At the **National Museum of Natural History**, you can also see rocks and minerals, stuffed birds and animals, skeletons and more! Have fun, Mate!

Below are 12 things you will see at this museum. Can you find them? Good luck, Mate!

ANIMAL	DIAMOND	TOPAZ
BEETLE	INSECTS	CRAB
BONE	GEM	DINOSAURS
CARAT	ROCK	ANTHILL

D	I	N	O	S	A	U	R	S
I	N	B	E	E	T	L	E	A
A	S	O	X	C	R	A	B	N
M	E	N	J	A	G	E	M	I
O	C	E	X	R	O	C	K	M
N	T	O	P	A	Z	X	B	A
D	S	A	N	T	H	I	L	L

A SPACED-OUT MUSEUM!

SPACED OUT!

The **National Air & Space Museum** is out-of-sight! There are airplanes, rockets, a Skylab Orbital Workshop, awesome movies, and more! You will want to take a tour of this museum because there is so much to see. To sign up for a tour and to find out what's happening at the museum that day, be sure to stop at the Information Desk as soon as you walk in.

Can you find the 19 hidden objects in the picture above? Good luck, Mate!

| sail boat | ruler | banana | frog | mushroom | fish | crown | pizza | lightning | snake |
| paint brush | pencil | knife | button | light bulb | hammer | nail | safety pin | fork |

COOL TOWER!

After walking around all of those neat museums, you must be starved! Me too, and I know just the place - **The Pavilion!**

The 2nd tallest building in D.C., the Old Post Office is now called "The Pavilion." It's a cool place! There's a clock tower to see, lots of food to eat and fun things to do!

Do NOT leave until you take a ride in the glass elevator to the top of the tower. **It's awesome!** A park ranger will give you a tour of the clock tower and show you the ropes that the bell ringers pull to make the 10 large bells ring in the tower.

What time is it when the clock strikes 13?!?!?

Time to fix the clock!!!

On Thursday evenings, you can hear the bells ring when the bell ringers practice.

 SPY - FBI!

The Federal Bureau of Investigation (FBI) tour is so interesting! See a video on the FBI, meet the "Ten Most Wanted Fugitives" and learn how FBI agents solve crimes.

Did you know that no 2 people in the world have the same fingerprints??? Not even identical twins!!!

Let's pretend we are detectives. Before we can solve the next case, we need an ID (identification) card. If you could design your own, what would it say and look like?

What did the mummy detective say when he solved the case?

That's a wrap!

HERE'S MY ID CARD!

DRAW YOUR ID CARD!

AGENT: _____

DISTINCTIVE MARKS:

EYES: ___
HEIGHT: ___
AGE: ___

#1 SPY

FINGERPRINTS

☆ SPECIAL FORCES ☆

FORD'S THEATRE!

Abraham Lincoln, the 16th President of the United States was shot on April 14, 1865 while watching a play at **Ford's Theatre**.

When you visit Ford's Theatre, you will see the Presidential box Lincoln was sitting in when he was shot. Then, go downstairs and visit the **Lincoln Museum**. It's really neat. You can see what President Lincoln was wearing that night, the gun that shot him, and more! When you finish, go across the street to the Petersen House. After President Lincoln was shot, he was carried over to the **Petersen House** where doctors cared for him until he died in the back bedroom the next morning. You will see the real pillow Lincoln slept on!

Here are 10 things you can see at Ford's Theatre. Can you help me find them? Good luck, Mate!

STAIN	SHOT	BOOTS
GUN	BLOOD	SEAT
TICKET	BOX	CLOTHES
	THEATRE	

T	I	C	K	E	T
H	B	L	O	O	D
E	B	O	O	T	S
A	S	T	A	I	N
T	H	H	G	U	N
R	O	E	B	O	X
E	T	S	E	A	T

31

A Fishy Museum!

Wow, this is the oldest aquarium in the United States! **The National Aquarium** first opened its doors to kids (and fish) in 1873.

It's over 100 years old! But don't worry Mate, the fish aren't. They are young and friendly. And, there are over 1,700 of them in 74 different tanks.

You can **touch** horseshoe crabs and snails in the Touch Tank, learn interesting facts about sharks, watch a neat movie at the Aquarium Theatre and lots more!

Be sure to check out the bookstore before you leave. If you want to **max-out on cool fish books**, this is the place!

Spell "5" things you can see here!

Where does a fish sleep?
In a water bed!

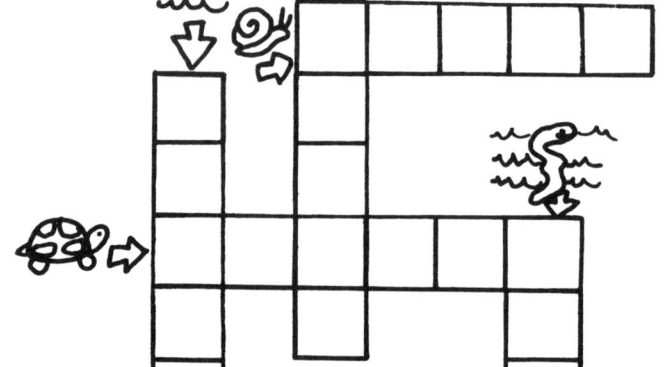

MY TRAVEL DIARY!

Washington, D.C. is awesome! I can't wait to tell my friends the neat things I have done so far. I better write and draw in my travel diary before I forget.

Dear Diary,

Today is _____.

Fun places I visited _____
_____
_____.

The most awesome thing I saw _____
_____

What I liked best _____
_____.

Draw 'n color

what I liked best!

It's my friend J.J. He's a **VIP** (Very Important Person)! He has arranged a VIK tour for me. I am so excited! And because you are a **VIK (Very Important Kid!)** you are also invited. Ready?

A VIK TOUR!

Here I am with my friend J.J. and my new friend, Morris. J.J. told me that a **VIK tour** is sooo special and lots of fun! You have a private guide who takes you to fun places and tells you awesome facts.

Today, **our guide is Morris**. He is a park ranger who gives tours to the "stars." He said he wanted to meet me because he and his daughter have read all of my books. Cool!

Well Mate, it's time to say good-bye to J.J. and start our VIK tour. Here's what we'll see.

We're off to visit Presidents, fun museums and my relatives! First stop, Washington Monument!

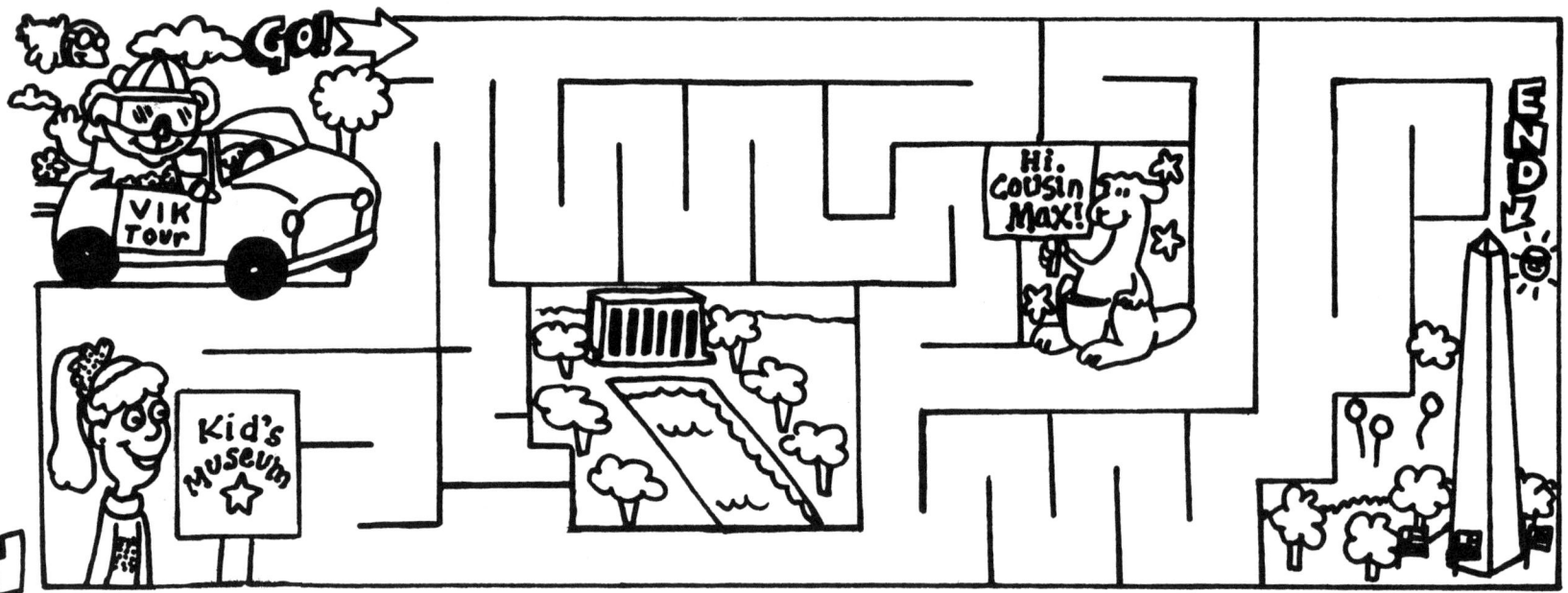

JUST FOR GEORGE!

Wow, it's the Washington Monument!

This is one of the United States' most famous memorials. A memorial is something that helps people remember a person or thing. This monument reminds us of the first President, George Washington.

Made out of white marble, it is the **tallest building in D.C.** and also one of the tallest buildings in the world! How tall? If you had to walk to the top, you would have to walk up 897 steps!

But thank goodness there is an elevator that takes you all the way to the top. The view from up here is awesome! I can see a lot of the famous places we have visited. I can even see the Lincoln Memorial which we are now going to visit. Follow us, Mate!

ON WITH THE TOUR!

Lincoln Memorial

Made out of white marble, this beautiful monument is as important and famous as **Abraham Lincoln** is!

As the 16th President, Abraham Lincoln was well known for a speech he made during the Civil War called the **Gettysburg Address**.

You can see this famous speech and also President Lincoln's second inaugural address carved on the walls of this monument.

Can you find the 16 hidden objects? Have fun and good luck, Mate!

heart   hot dog   toothpaste   worm   lemon slice   arrow   butterfly   money
toothbrush   paper clip   cup   hanger   ice cream cone   fork   pie slice   fish

♥ WE WILL REMEMBER ♥

Welcome to **Arlington National Cemetery** - the largest military cemetery in the world! President Kennedy is buried here. Over his grave you will see the eternal flame. "Eternal" means it will never go out. It burns forever so we will always remember him.

On the hill, you can visit the **Arlington House**, a memorial to Robert E. Lee (a famous general during the Civil War) and also see the resting place of D.C.'s architect, Pierre L'Enfant.

And don't leave until you visit the **Tomb of the Unknowns**! In memory of missing soldiers from three wars, a guard marches back and forth in their honor. Every hour, there is a changing of the guard. The guard walks forward 21 steps, stops for 21 seconds and then walks back 21 steps. Morris told me the guard does not look at a watch, but counts the 21 seconds in his head. Awesome!

A COOL STATUE!

We are now at the **Jefferson Memorial**. What a cool statue! Thomas Jefferson, the 3rd President of the United States wrote the Declaration of Independence which gave the U.S. its freedom from England.

You probably knew that, but did you know that Thomas Jefferson was a famous architect? He designed the Virginia Capitol, the University of Virginia and his own home, Monticello.

Now, want to learn something that very few people know? **Look behind Thomas Jefferson**. Near the bottom, you will see corn and tobacco carved into this bronze statue. Ask your parents if they knew this. Yesss! You are so smart!

MAX'S FACTS!
The Declaration of Independence was signed July 4, 1776. Now, July 4th is a national holiday and is celebrated with food, fun & fireworks!

What did the big firecracker say to the little firecracker?
My pop's bigger than yours!

YOU ARE SOOO SMART

Wow, we have learned so much! Before we go on, here are a few more questions to test your memory. O.K. Mate, put on your thinking cap! Without peeking, **circle your answer** and when you finish, turn to the page listed to see how you did. **Good luck!**

1. The only woman to appear on U.S. paper money was:
   Betsy Ross   OR   Madonna   OR   Martha Washington   (Page 23)

2. Thomas Jefferson, 3rd President of the U.S. wrote:
   Rock Music   OR   Declaration of Independence   OR   Gettysburg Address   (Page 38)

3. The world's largest living land animals are:
   Dinosaurs   OR   African Bush Elephants   OR   Whales   (Page 26)

4. Identical twins have fingerprints that are:
   Different   OR   Identical   OR   Similar   (Page 30)

5. The Star-Spangled Banner is a:
   Flag   OR   National anthem   OR   Both of these   (Page 25)

6. Can you name these buildings:

(Page 16)

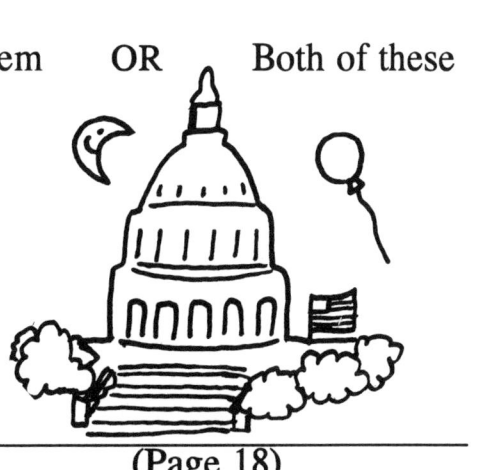
(Page 18)

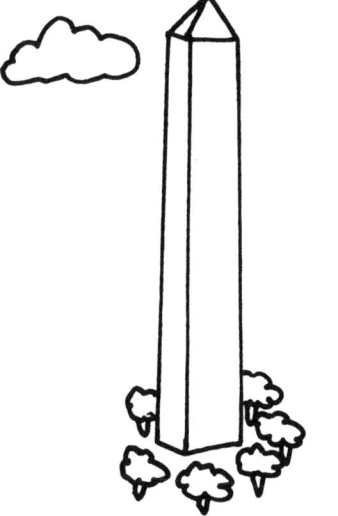
(Page 35)

IT'S WORLDLY!

ONE MINUTE UNTIL BLAST OFF!

A small museum, but a cool one, is **Explorers Hall at the National Geographic Society!**

Here you will see exhibits that teach you about earth, geography and outer space!

My favorite one is Earth Station One! Watch the huge globe of the world. When it starts moving, it's time to enter the Earth Station One Theatre.

Once you are seated, you will blast off on an orbital flight that takes you 23,000 miles above earth. It's awesome, Mate!

LEAVING EARTH IN ONE MINUTE

Before we blast off, can you help me find the 12 hidden words below? Good luck!

Station   Air   Globe
People   Sun   Rocks
Moon   Land   Stars
Water   Earth
Exhibit

A	I	R	J	G	I	L
P	E	O	P	L	E	A
N	X	C	W	O	A	N
S	H	K	A	B	R	D
T	I	S	T	E	T	M
A	B	U	E	M	H	O
R	I	N	R	A	X	O
S	T	A	T	I	O	N

A KID'S MUSEUM!

Welcome to The Capital Children's Museum! This is a cool museum just for kids! There are so many fun things to see and do here. And, you can **touch** everything. There is a Computer Hall, TV Studio, Storyteller Theatre and more! There is even a Mexican Hall where you can make and taste Mexican tortillas and hot chocolate. Yummy! I'm starved, so let's go eat and play.

Follow me Mate, as we take a tour of this cool museum, just for kids!

COOL ZOO!

This is it, Mate, our last stop! What an awesome way to end our tour, at a cool zoo - **National Zoo!** There are so many fun things to see and do here.

What's first? Check out the Education Building to find out what's happening. Then it's off to Amazonia! Here you can pretend you are on the Amazon River where you will see a rain forest, fish, insects, birds and meet Dr. Brazil!

Later, visit the gang at the Ape House, Bird House, House of Reptiles, Beaver Valley and my spineless friends at the Invertebrate Exhibit!

Can you spell the names of 7 animals you can find at this zoo?

Say hi to my kangaroo cousins! How are we related? First of all, **I am not a bear!** Koalas and kangaroos belong to a group of mammals called **marsupials** (mar-soup-ē-els). We all have a pouch on our stomach where we carry our relatives and cool shades!

Good-bye, D.C.!

A surprise party! Yesss! J.J. and Morris planned it. They wanted the last stop of our **VIK** tour to be celebrated with friends and relatives. What a great way to say good-bye to Washington, D.C.!

Before we leave the National Zoo, can you find the 15 hidden objects below? Good luck, Mate!

| fork | button | scissors | light bulb | cup | arrow | sunglasses | fish |
| comb | ruler | paper clip | band aid | ring | heart | paint brush | |

43

GOOD-BYE, MATE!

I am sooo sad. I cannot believe that it's time to say good-bye. Touring Washington, D.C., has been such an awesome experience! Before we leave, let's write and draw in our travel diary.

Dear Diary,

Today is _____.

Fun places I visited _____
_____
_____.

The most awesome thing I saw _____
_____

What I liked best _____
_____.

Draw 'N Color

What I liked best!

Well Mate, the tour is over, but the fun isn't. On pages 45 and 46, there's important information for your parents. On page 47, there's important information for **you** about my **VIK** Club!

PARENT GUIDE

ARLINGTON NATIONAL CEMETERY (703) 692-0931, Arlington, VA 22211. Daily: October-March, 8am-5pm; April-September, 8am-7pm. FREE. **Illustrated on page 37**.

ARTS AND INDUSTRIES BUILDING (202) 357-1481; **Discovery Theatre** (202) 357-1500, 900 Jefferson Drive, SW 20560. One of 14 museums that make up the Smithsonian Institution. Here kids will see a collection of Victorian Americana. Daily: 10am-5:30pm, (spring/summer hours vary). Closed Christmas. FREE. October-June, the Discovery Theatre is open. Admission. Not illustrated.

BUREAU OF ENGRAVING AND PRINTING (202) 622-2000, 14th and C Streets, SW 20228. Open: Monday-Friday, 9am-2pm. Self-guided tour. FREE. Closed federal holidays and the week of Christmas. **Illustrated on page 23**.

CAPITAL CHILDREN'S MUSEUM (202) 543-8600; (202) MET-KIDS (tape), 800 3rd Street, NE, 20002. Daily: 10am-5pm. Closed national holidays. Admission. **Illustrated on page 41**.

CAPITOL, U.S. (202) 224-3121; (202) 225-6827 (tours), National Mall (East End) 20510. Daily: 9am-8pm. Half-hour tours: 9am-3:45pm. FREE. Closed Thanksgiving, Christmas and New Year's Day. **Illustrated on page 18**.

FEDERAL BUREAU OF INVESTIGATION (202) 324-3447, J. Edgar Hoover Building, E Street (between 9th and 10th Streets, NW) 20535. Open: Monday-Friday, 8:45am-4:15pm. One-hour tour. FREE. Closed federal holidays. **Illustrated page 30**.

FORD'S THEATRE & LINCOLN MUSEUM (202) 426-6924, 511 10th Street, NW 20004. Daily: 9am-5pm. FREE. Closed Christmas and during matinees. **Illustrated on page 31**.

FREDERICK DOUGLASS' HOME (202) 426-5961, 1411 W Street, SE 20020. Home of the famous black abolitionist and author. Daily: 9am-4pm; (April 15-October 15 until 5pm). FREE. Closed Thanksgiving, Christmas and New Year's Day. Not illustrated.

JEFFERSON MEMORIAL (202) 426-6841, Tidal Basin (South Bank), West Potomac Park. Daily: 24 hours. Tours from 8am-midnight. FREE. Closed Christmas. **Illustrated on page 38**.

LIBRARY OF CONGRESS (202) 707-5458, 10 First Street, SE, 20540. Guided half-hour tours are available. FREE. Open: Monday-Friday, 8:30am-9:30pm; Saturday & Sunday, 8:30am-6pm. Closed Christmas and New Year's Day. **Illustrated on page 19**.

LINCOLN MEMORIAL (202) 426-6841, West Potomac Park at 23rd Street, NW. Daily: 24 hours. Tours conducted upon request from 8am-midnight. FREE. Closed Christmas. **Illustrated on page 36**.

METRORAIL/METROBUS (202) 637-7000, call for times and route information. **Illustrated on page 15**.

MOUNT VERNON (703) 780-2000, Mount Vernon, VA 22121. The former home of George Washington, 14 rooms of this beautiful house are open to the public. Daily: 9am-4pm (March-October to 5pm). Admission. Not illustrated.

NATIONAL AIR AND SPACE MUSEUM (202) 357-1400), 6th Street & Independence Avenue, SW 20560. Daily: 10am-5:30pm (spring/summer hours vary). FREE. Great cafeteria. Closed Christmas. **Illustrated on page 28**.

NATIONAL AQUARIUM (202)482-2825, U.S. Department of Commerce Bldg, 14th Street & Constitution Avenue, NW 20230. Open daily, 9am-5pm. ADMISSION. Closed Christmas. **Illustrated on page 32**.

PARENT GUIDE

NATIONAL ARCHIVES (202) 501-5240, 8th Street & Constitution Avenue, NW 20408. Bill of Rights, Declaration of Independence and the Constitution are on public display. Daily: 10am-5:30pm (April 1-Labor Day, until 9pm). FREE. Closed Christmas. Not illustrated.

NATIONAL GEOGRAPHIC SOCIETY EXPLORERS HALL (202) 857-7588, 17th & M Streets, NW 20036. Daily: 10am- 5:30pm (spring/summer hours vary). FREE. Closed Christmas. **Illustrated on page 40**.

NATIONAL MUSEUM OF AMERICAN HISTORY (202) 357-2700; (202) 357-1481 (tours), 14th Street & Constitution Avenue, NW 20560. Daily: 10am-5:30pm (spring/summer hours vary). FREE. Closed Christmas. **Illustrated on page 25.**

NATIONAL MUSEUM OF NATURAL HISTORY (202) 357-2747, 10th Street & Constitution Avenue, NW 20560. Daily: 10am-5:30pm (spring/summer hours vary). FREE. Closed Christmas. **Illustrated on pages 27 & 28.**

NATIONAL ZOOLOGICAL PARK (202) 673-4717; (202) 673-4800 (tape), 3000 block of Connecticut Avenue, NW 20008. Daily: April 1-October 15: grounds (8am-8pm), buildings (9am-6pm); October 16-March 31: grounds (8am-6pm), buildings (10am-4:30pm). FREE. Closed Christmas. **Illustrated on pages 42 & 43.**

PAVILION - AT THE OLD POST OFFICE (202) 289-4224, 1100 Pennsylvania Avenue, NW 20004. Clock tower is open daily: October-March, 10am-5:45pm; April-September, 8am-10:45pm. (Thursdays closed from 6:30pm-9:30pm for bell ringing). Pavilion is open daily 10am-6pm (spring/summer hours vary). FREE. Food Court opens earlier. **Illustrated page 29**.

PETERSEN HOUSE (202) 426-6830, 516 10th Street, NW 20004. Daily: 9am-5pm. FREE. Closed Christmas. **Illustrated page 31**.

SMITHSONIAN INSTITUTION BUILDING - THE CASTLE (202) 357-2700; (202)357-2020 (taped events) 1000 Jefferson Drive SW 20560. Visitor Center. Daily: 9am-5pm (spring/summer hours vary). FREE. Closed Christmas. **Illustrated page 24**.

SUPREME COURT, U.S. (202) 479-3000; First & East Capitol Streets, NW 20543. Monday-Friday, 9am-4:30pm. Court is in session two weeks of every month (October-April). Tours: 9am-3:30 pm, Monday-Friday, when Court is not in session. FREE. Closed federal holidays and weekends. **Illustrated on page 19**.

UNION STATION (202) 289-1908; (202)371-9441, 40 Massachusetts Avenue, NE. One block north from the Capitol Building, this historic and majestic landmark, now houses 120 stores, shops, restaurants and a nine-screen movie theatre. Open Monday-Saturday, 10am-9pm; Sunday, noon-6pm. Closed Christmas, Thanksgiving, Easter, New Year's Day. Not illustrated.

VIETNAM VETERANS MEMORIAL (202) 426-6841, Constitution Avenue between Henry Bacon Drive & 21st Street, NW. Daily: 24 hours. FREE. Not illustrated.

WASHINGTON MONUMENT (202) 426-6841, On National Mall at 15th Street, NW. Daily: 9am-5pm (April 1-Labor Day, until midnight). FREE. Closed Christmas. **Illustrated on page 35**.

WHITE HOUSE (202)456-2200; (202) 456-7041, 1600 Pennsylvania Avenue, NW 20500. Tuesday-Saturday, 10am-noon. FREE. Closed Sunday, Monday, Christmas, New Year's Day and for Presidential functions. **Illustrated on pages 16 & 17.**

MAX'S VIK CLUB!

Here it is Mate, the information you have been waiting for. To join my **VIK (Very Important Kid!) Club**, return the Frequent Reader Coupon to my address below. As soon as I receive it, I will send you your very own **VIK card**! When you mail me your coupon, please tell me what you liked best about this book. Also, I need silly riddles. Thanks, Mate!

Well Mate, it's time for me to return to Australia to write my next book. Thanks for traveling with me. Have a safe trip home. I'll miss you!

Your friend,

MAX
23015 Del Lago Drive
Suite D2-172
Laguna Hills, California 92653

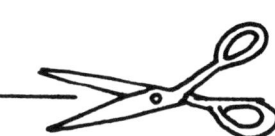

FREQUENT READER COUPON

Hurry! Mail today to receive your **VIK card**!

I traveled with MAX to _____

My name is _____ Age _____ Grade _____

Address (Street) _____

City _____ State _____ Zip _____